Dear Parents,

A love of reading is something we wish for every child. This book series is designed to encourage reading—with entry points appropriate to most any reader. Our well-defined levels help you choose books that are best suited to your child's interests and ability. These colorful books tap into a child's imagination and build confidence for a lifelong love of reading.

Our Read Smart bookmarks reinforce your child's reading vocabulary through games and activities. Take the time to make reading more fun by following the simple instructions on the bookmark.

Reading is a voyage that can take your child into wonderful, enchanting places. We are delighted to join you on this journey.

 BEGINNING READER

For children who are ready to read their first books, know their letter sounds, and have developed an understanding of early phonics skills. Words include short vowels, simple plurals, and sight words.

 DEVELOPING READER

For children who are ready for longer sentences and more lines of print per page. Stories are richer and include a growing vocabulary. Words feature beginning consonant blends.

 CONFIDENT READER

For children who are ready for books with longer sentences and richer plots. Words are longer and feature ending consonant blends and simple suffixes.

 ADVANCED READER

For children who are ready for books with more complex plots, varied sentence structure, and full paragraphs. Words feature long vowels and vowel combinations.

ISBN 1-60143-977-6

Over My Head

Written by **Russell Ginns**
Illustrated by **Andy Norman**

I am Lou.

I had a big day.

Now I want to go to bed.

I take off my hat.

I slip off my socks.

Then I hop into the tub.

I stop all the drips.

I get snug in my bed,

but I hear TAP, TAP, TAP!

Is Denzel up there?

I bet he is!

I call him and say,

"What are you up to?

I want to sleep."

"Hi, Pal," he says to me.

"I like to tap on pots and pans.

Do you want to tap with me?"

"I want to sleep. When you go TAP, TAP, TAP, I cannot sleep. Please stop."

"OK, Pal," he says.

"I will stop."

"Thank you," I say.

So I go back to bed.

Then I hear CLICK, CLICK, CLACK!

I call to Denzel and say,

"What was that?"

"Hi, Lou," he says.

"I like to stack bricks."

"I can stack them up. Then they drop. Do you want to stack bricks with me?"

"No, I do not want to play with bricks. I want to sleep. When you go CLICK, CLICK, CLACK, I cannot sleep. Please stop."

"OK, I will stop," says Denzel.

"Thank you," I say.

I go back to bed.

Will I hear a TAP?

Will I hear a CLACK?

Now I can get to sleep.

QUACK!
QUACK!
THUD!

I get out of bed.

I go up to see Denzel.

"What was that?" I ask.

"Hi, Lou," he says.

"Do you like this game? I play it with ducks. I can flip them into a box. Do you want to flip a duck too?"

"No!" I yell.

"I do not want to flip a duck!

When you go QUACK, QUACK,

THUD, I cannot sleep."

"Do you not like ducks?" asks Denzel.

"I do like ducks.

But I want to go to bed!"

"I do not want to hear a TAP or a CLACK. Do not make a CLICK or a QUACK or a THUD! You must stop now!"

"Well, OK," he says.

"I will stop. I will go to sleep now too."

At last there is no TAP or CLICK.

I do not hear a CLACK or QUACK or

THUD. I can sleep.

COCK-A-DOODLE-DOO!